For
G<sub></sub>

# DARKSIDE SEATTLE:
# FIXER

# DARKSIDE SEATTLE:
# FIXER

## L.E. FRENCH

Published by Clockwork Dragon Books

clockworkdragon.net

First printing, June 2017

Copyright © 2017 by Lee French

ISBN: 978-1-944334-17-8

*For Josh, Chimi, and Ruben. None of you play cyberpunk games with me, but you're awesome anyway.*

# CHAPTER 1

At thirteen minutes past three in the afternoon, I activated the illegal jammer on the dashboard of my hovercar. The black box, too big to fit in my suit pocket, prevented the WAINet from noticing when I took the steering wheel and left approved flight lanes, as well as blocking the GPS signal from my government-mandated cranial implant. Once freed from surveillance, I drove the car down, into Darkside Seattle.

I skimmed streets for several blocks in light drizzle, in case any cops had seen me dive in. Rubble lined side streets, telephone poles had long ago been downed and salvaged, and every store window had been boarded up or bricked over. Weeds grew in cracks. Ridges in the asphalt and concrete showed the location of roots belonging to large, leafy trees allowed to grow unchecked. Mold clung to the old plaster facades of rundown buildings.

Like most good Seattleites, I spent as little time in

DeeSeat as possible. Like an entirely different kind of Seattleite, I kept a gun in the storage pod near my feet for such visits.

By the time I reached the old, ruined football stadium parking lot, my contact leaned against a jagged chunk of concrete the size of a boulder. His sharp, dark trench coat, the collar turned up against the early March chill, fit into DeeSeat as well as my luxury sports car and silver silk suit did. He looked up with a wary smile as my car neared him.

The moment I stopped, he dashed for the passenger side door and slid inside. I curled my lip as his damp ass hit the real leather seat. If he sat for long, he'd damage the material.

"It's colder than fuck today." After digging in his pocket for a moment, he produced a box wrapped in blank paper, about eight inches long, two inches deep, and four inches wide.

I took the box and tapped the dash readout to turn up the heat for him. Warm, dry air blasted his face. He sighed with pleasure. Though I'd already drank half of it, I offered him my coffee in its artificially heated plastic mug.

"You're a fucking angel, Godhand." He gripped the cup with both hands and slurped.

Smirking, I glanced into the rearview mirror, watching for cops. We could've used someplace with more cover, but I liked the escape options of open space. Besides, deeper into DeeSeat meant more chances to be murdered for my car. "Nice to see you too, Jay."

He leaned against the seat. "My jammer's busted. I had to fucking walk here from Occidental."

"When did that happen?" His job required a jammer. Without one, I considered him useless. My people needed full functionality on a moment's notice.

"A few days ago. Conked out in the middle of a run to Puyallup. Had to detour, took five times as long to get anything done." He held up a hand. "New one is on order already. Twiddle doesn't have any on hand."

"Sounds like Twiddle needs some competition. Did you check with Pigwig?"

Frowning at the coffee mug, he shook his head. "Didn't think to. I guess that's why you make the big bucks, Boss Lady. I'll check with him tonight."

"Good. While you're doing that, I need a functional scale model of an 1802 Trevithick locomotive engine made by hand from die-cast metal. With it, I want a bar of Swiss chocolate shaped like an old-fashioned train. Any kind of steam engine is fine."

Jay raised an eyebrow. "That shit's legal. Marie could've handled that. I mean, I know that box isn't legal, but it's wrapped in paper. We could've met downtown. I could've waited for you in my car. My warm, dry car."

"Marie couldn't find either without a two-month minimum wait. I need them faster than that. And meeting downtown leads to me being connected with you, and you know it." I watched an old-fashioned motorcycle rumble past on two wheels. "Besides, there's one more thing. A cute little engineering firm called BowerTech is developing a prototype for the next generation in solar cells."

"Steal it or blow it up?"

"Steal everything." The company had already rebuffed my father's efforts to buy it. Twice.

"Got it, Boss. Anything else?"

I started to shake my head, then stopped. The next step in the train plan needed a timetable. "How long do you think the train things will take?"

Jay sipped his coffee. "I don't even know what a trevifuck is."

"Trevithick."

"Yeah, that. Could be a day, could be I have to

commission some asshole to make it. Does it have to be authentic or anything? If I have to get a forgery—"

"No, it can be new. The chocolate had better be Swiss, though."

Jay grumbled under his breath. "I'll check around and pass Marie a note about timeframe as soon as I've got one."

"Good enough." I gave the door a meaningful look.

"Aw, c'mon. It's fucking freezing out there. At least give me a ride halfway."

I liked Jay. He did good work. But we had rules for a reason. "Sorry. Can't risk it."

"Yeah, yeah. I'll see you soon." He opened the door.

"Bill me for the new jammer."

"Yes, ma'am." Grinning, he slammed the door shut and flipped me a salute.

I backed away from him, turned the car around, and skimmed through the streets again before lurching into the air. As soon as I neared a hovering buoy-marked flight lane, I shut off the jammer and activated the autopilot. The car merged into the shiny ribbon of hovercars streaming over the south end of Seattle at two hundred feet.

Less than two miles from the shittiest part of the city, towers of plassteel loomed over a glitzy downtown that would sparkle if the sun ever shined. Traffic skimmed around the cluster of skyscrapers at four different levels with thin streams diving into and out of each stream. My car followed an exit path until it reached my father's building.

As it touched down on a lighted perch at the twenty-third floor, I scanned the messages collected by my cranial implant. Fifteen highway ads in my inbox went straight to the trash. Another thirty had been automatically filtered there.

The car slid toward the building on a conveyor belt. In front of me, a wide door slid upward and lights flickered on. My car slipped into a sleek, white frame. As soon as it stopped, the garage door closed and I stepped out of the car. I followed the short walkway to an interior door that opened for me. Behind me, the frame whirred to lift my car into the ceiling and prepare for the next vehicle.

As Godhand International Incorporated's Executive Vice President of Risk Management and Chief Nepotism Officer, I could use the limo anytime I wanted, of course. But the limo lacked a self-drive option. Besides, the big, black car also stood out much more than a silver sports car.

Two department head messages scrolled across the bottom of my vision in green letters. Neither needed immediate attention. I rode the express elevator to the lobby.

The ride from the twenty-third floor took less than a minute. When the elevator doors opened into the huge, airy space, I stepped out and checked for the person I needed to see.

My heels clacked on the green-veined faux marble floor. We could've put in genuine marble, but Dad didn't see a reason to waste that much money when he could blow it on a granite waterfall and fountain instead. Tropical plants grew from the fountain and spotlights augmented the perpetually weak, gray sunlight balking at the huge wall of glass facing the street outside. Screens on the rest of the walls provided directory and map assistance for visitors who chose to walk in the front doors.

I smiled as I spotted my target. GIInc. employed hundreds of thousands of people around the world, and about ten thousand in this building. Of those on the premises, about one thousand worked for me, either directly or through department heads. When it came to recognizing employees personally, I kept my appearances to major milestones and let Marie send everyone cards or flowers for routine observances like birthdays or anniversaries.

The security guard I aimed for straightened as I approached. He stood at attention beside the front door. Though his uniform could have been crisper, I didn't care.

Under the circumstances, the man looked good. Nervous, but good.

"Dave," I said, handing him Jay's box, "I'd like to congratulate you on the recent birth of your first child."

He relaxed and smiled as he took the box containing two genuine Cuban cigars. They'd become challenging to acquire after West America outlawed tobacco. "Oh. Thank you, ma'am. We got the flowers you sent. They were really nice."

"I'm glad you and your wife liked them." I leaned in and murmured, "Don't open the box in public."

"Oh. Yes, ma'am. Thank you." He tucked the box into his back pocket.

We shook hands.

"Truth be told, ma'am, I'm kind of happy to be back to work."

I grinned, partially because his fate awaited me in the not too distant future. "We're happy to have you back." With that, I patted him on the shoulder and returned to the elevator. Next stop, the executive floor where both my Dad and I kept our offices.

# CHAPTER 2

The elevator doors opened to a reception area with plush, beige carpet, white walls, and glittering golden fixtures. My father's hand-picked, thirty-something protégé blocked most of my view and all of my path with his broad shoulders and broader ego. Ross's steel gray suit mimicked my preference for silver, something he did on purpose.

I watched his dark eyes flick down my body, then up to meet my gaze as if he hadn't ogled me. "Vickie," he said as a greeting. "I'm off to visit the Gray's Harbor facility. Meet me for dinner?"

"Busy tonight." I took a step toward him, hoping he'd move.

Instead of getting out of my way, he slipped an arm around me and slid his hand to my ass. His cologne, applied a touch too heavily, assaulted my nose. "You're always busy."

"That's true. It's because I work here." As much as I

enjoyed verbal sparring with Ross, I shuffled to turn us around. At least he didn't resist me. Maybe the knowledge that my father's secretary, Viola, watched us had something to do with that.

Ross squeezed my ass before letting go. He should've admired my restraint, because I didn't knee him in the balls. Someday, when I controlled the company, I'd fire Ross. He'd get a severance package and go find another job where he could bang his secretary without bothering me. He needed a woman who cooed over his pretty face instead of someone who only wanted to smash it.

"All work and no play makes for an empty life," Ross said.

I ignored him and smiled at Viola. She nodded, probably handling five messages at once. With her acknowledgment, I breezed into my father's office. Gold and real wood decorated the spacious office. If he wanted to, Dad could live here. Between the wet bar, giant bathroom, and squashy couch along one wall, he had everything he needed. Some nights, he did stay here.

This afternoon, he sat behind his imposing cherry desk, tapping on a tablet. He glanced at me, smiled, and set his tablet aside. Reaching under his desk, he flicked a switch.

It clicked. Green letters scrolled across the bottom of my vision without my consent.

[VictoriaGodhandSystem: WAINet signal lost. Attempting to re-establish network connection.]

Dad had activated the office's wide-band jammer. Neither of our implants could overcome that. While waiting for them to give up, I sat in the leather wingback chair opposite Dad.

[VictoriaGodhandSystem: Unable to re-establish WAINet connection. Entering offline mode. Recommend changing location by at least 100 feet or exiting the current structure.]

Dad gestured to his tablet. "I just got a report about BezOhben. You wouldn't have anything to do with that, would you?"

"The CFO has a thing for blondes." I tapped my platinum hair, taking care not to disturb the bun I'd wrapped it into.

He raised an eyebrow. "You didn't screw him, did you?"

"No." Not that it was any of his business. "He's eighty years old. That's gross. I reminded him of his granddaughter, so I rolled with it. With his access, I was able to get one of my people hired there, and now we have an espionage funnel."

"Excellent." He leaned back in his chair, broadcasting paternal pride. "Ready or not, we're playing with the big boys now. Any luck with the extraterritoriality yet?"

"I finally got someone to tell me what Figueroa would like as a gift. As soon as I have those things in hand, I'll schedule a meeting. Him, I'll probably have to screw." His wife, Lucia, I had a feeling, would want to watch or participate. She'd told me far too much about her husband, and stared far too long at my breasts for casual interest.

Dad snorted like he thought I was joking. I let him think that. "Make sure you get me anything you need signed by Friday."

I'd forgotten about his annual trip to the site of his and Mom's honeymoon next week. Whenever possible, I forgot about Mom and all the special dates associated with her. Her funeral had closed a book in my life, and I preferred for it to stay that way.

"Beyond that, I want you to make some time for Ross."

"What?" The new subject blindsided me. "Ross? He doesn't have anything to do with this."

"No, but he's our COO."

"And? My job doesn't involve him."

"Victoria," he chided, using a tone I hated. With a simple inflection of my name, he made me feel like a fifteen-year-old caught sneaking out to see a sleazy boyfriend.

"What?"

Dad pursed his lips and steepled his fingers. Combined with his silver hair and impeccable suit, he reminded me of a corporate villain from the vids. "We've known him and his family for decades. He's talented, he doesn't need the money, and you'd be a good fit with him."

I forced my face blank. The other option? Throwing up. "I'll take that under advisement."

"I know you've been dodging him, and I don't see why. You're both smart, attractive professionals. You have similar interests and goals."

Nothing else mattered, of course. "I'm not really interested in him."

"You know, you were already four when your mother was thirty-one. Don't you have that biological clock urge?"

We stared at each other. I considered the best way to shut down this conversation.

"Do you want me to fuck him on your desk?"

He grimaced. "Please don't."

"Then stop talking about this."

"I'm only asking you to give him a chance."

I stood. "I'm going to ask Viola to schedule a harassment seminar for you. This isn't an appropriate conversation for business hours."

"Fine, fine." He held up his hands in surrender. "I'm dropping it." Picking up his tablet, he pointed at me. "For now."

"I don't want to hear about this at work again." My words came out more distant and harsh than I intended. Rather than let myself apologize, I turned my back on him and walked away.

"I'm only interested in what's best for you."

The men in my life always seemed to need to get the last word in.

# CHAPTER 3

[MarieSclavo: ETA on the trains is Sunday. The other matter has a tentative timeline of one week, but it's expected to slip. I also have an invoice for a piece of vehicle equipment?]

[VictoriaGodhand: Good. Pay the invoice.] I breezed down the hall to my office. Jay worked fast, a trait I appreciated and rewarded.

As soon as I reached my office, Marie jumped to her feet and followed me inside with a tablet in hand. She wore my favorite red suit. The skirt clung to her hips and hit her an inch above her knees, making her legs seem a mile long. My favorite part? Her tailored jacket had a false shell instead of a blouse. When she slipped out of it, only her bra remained. Marie had excellent taste in lingerie.

Marie shut the door. Where my father could live in his office, I actually did live in mine. After four months of late-night meetings and calls had brought me into work at odd hours, I'd given up my apartment. As a side benefit, the door locked. One simple system command to the building gave me complete privacy.

The spacious corner office had been divided into two rooms. Unlike my father, I preferred smaller spaces. My workspace consisted of a small standing desk and touchscreen access point for the central computing system, along with four armchairs and a couch around a coffee table. Most of the work I did on the premises involved chatting and coffee. Sometimes, it involved the bed in the next room.

"Senator Gates messaged to accept your invitation tonight. He'll be here at six."

Though Marie stifled most of it, I caught the ghost of a pout around her mouth as she tapped on her tablet. She used it to handle matters through company accounts, which provided a degree of anonymity not possible through implants. Everything with Jay went through one of those accounts.

Pausing with my hand on the knob for my bedroom suite, I beckoned her closer. She shuffled to my side. I slipped an arm around her waist and kissed her.

We kept our relationship secret to protect Marie.

Corporate espionage and sabotage happened, as my job attested, and people knowing about my affair with my secretary put her at risk. I couldn't give her up, so I protected her with every tool in my arsenal.

When I broke off the kiss, Marie sighed and leaned against me. "I hate it when you take meetings with him."

I tugged her into the bedroom and shut the door behind us before wrapping my arms around her. With my implant's connection to the suite's private node, I commanded the screens I had instead of walls to shift from our usual neutral decor to a soft pink color scheme. "I know. It's not exactly fun for me either."

"You could quit. We could start a consulting firm. Hire some other women to do that part. Ones that would like it."

"I work for my dad, not some random asshole. Besides, you want to have a baby. Can't do that and start a new company at the same time. Come on, help me change."

Marie sighed. "I don't want you to change."

I chuckled and kissed her cheek. "I love you too."

With another sigh, Marie let go of me to flump on the bed. I went into my closet wondering what excuse Senator Gates gave his wife to explain his late meetings with me. She probably had no idea how much naughtiness her husband participated in. Or maybe she knew and accepted it.

Silver dominated the suits and evening gowns hanging on the rack. Passing them, I headed for my lingerie collection. None of that section involved gray or silver. Gates's favorite slip and robe hung on the end.

"Do you want me to order dinner?" Marie called from the bed.

"Hors d'oeuvres and desserts."

A message from Ross pinged in my vision. I grimaced and took the lingerie from its hangar.

[RossLynch: Reconsider dinner with me tonight.]

[VictoriaGodhand: I told you, I'm busy. I have a late meeting.]

[RossLynch: Tomorrow. Or Friday. You can't have a late meeting then. No one works on Friday nights.]

I laughed out loud. Ross didn't know shit about my job. If I had my way, that would never change. At some point, I really needed to get some dirt on him. That would, of course, never happen if I never led him on. Maybe I needed to get over my revulsion and meet with him. Dad would think I'd listened to reason and stop lecturing me, at least.

Tossing my suit jacket aside, I sucked it up to do the

thing. "Do I have anything scheduled for tomorrow evening?"

Marie appeared at the closet door. "No."

"Block out my night, starting at five."

[VictoriaGodhand: Tomorrow is fine. I'll be ready at five.]

[RossLynch: Excellent.] The smugness permeated his text, though that might've been my imagination.

"What're you doing tomorrow?" Marie asked.

"Having dinner with Ross."

She grimaced while I unzipped my skirt and shimmied out of it. "Seriously?"

"Yes, seriously."

"But you hate him. I hate him. Everybody hates him."

I sighed and pulled off my blouse. "I've done worse."

"I don't think hiring out wetwork is worse than having sex with Ross."

Chuckling, I faced the only person in the world I trusted with my life. My father didn't rate as high as Marie. "I'm not going to have sex with him." I pressed a quick kiss on her lips. "That would just encourage him. I'm taking a one-on-one, after-hours meeting with him to see if I can discover any weaknesses to exploit."

"That's not how things work with men," she said. "If it has even the tiniest whiff of being a date, he'll get worse."

"It's not a date. It's just dinner."

"That's how slasher vids begin." She picked up my jacket and skirt, and deposited them in the dry cleaning bag near the door.

I snorted and stripped off my underwear. Marie leaned against the wall and watched, her gaze drifting across my body. For her benefit, I took my time with the pink lace slip and satin robe.

"You look terrible in pink." Marie said that every time she saw me in this getup.

"I'll wear whatever you want tomorrow, because when I'm done with him, I'm coming home to you."

"Ew. No. Not if there's a chance Ross might see it. Wear a sports bra and granny underpants for him. Save the nice undies for that dinner party on Saturday."

Laughing, I stepped into matching low-heel slippers. I reviewed my internal memo notes about what Gates liked and hated. Mixing these men's preferences never turned out well. One wrong move and a contract got stuck in committee.

Because I loved her, I shuffled to Marie and held her.

I wanted to let my hands wander, but had work to do tonight. Besides, the lace grated against her sensitive skin. Marie preferred silk and satin.

"The food you wanted is here already." Marie produced a custom, form-fitted mask and pressed it to my face. The device removed my work makeup and applied delicate pink shades across my face. Senator Gates wanted a sweet girl, not a whore. "Gates just landed. He's on his way up."

I took her chin. "Go do something fun. I'll message you when he leaves."

Marie nodded and touched my hand. "See you soon." She left me, returning to her station outside my office. She'd wait there until Gates arrived, let him in, and leave. Another message from Ross flashed in my notifications.

[RossLynch: You're having dinner with Senator Gates? Shouldn't I be in on that meeting?]

[VictoriaGodhand: No.]

[RossLynch: As the COO, I think I should be included in a meeting with someone as important as a senator.]

I wanted to punch him in the face. Why was he even in the building at this hour?

[VictoriaGodhand: I don't tell you how to do your job or interfere with your meetings, and I expect the same courtesy in return. Leave him alone and stay away from my meeting.]

[RossLynch: Vickie. You're not at the same level as me. You don't get to tell me what to do.]

The gall of him to pull rank. He knew my job title had nothing to do with my seniority. I'd been part of the company a decade longer than him. Still, I needed to keep things civil. Yelling at him or insulting him might cause him to storm into my office, and I didn't need him to see me in this stupid pink getup.

[VictoriaGodhand: Do you want to have dinner with me tomorrow night or not? Let me do my job or that evening is cancelled because I'll be spending it trying to fix the damage you cause by refusing to let me handle this my way. If you're looking to gladhand powerful people, I can set you up with a dinner party, but you do not appropriate my meetings for your purposes.]

His next message took almost a minute to arrive.

[RossLynch: I see your point. I'll talk to you tomorrow.]

He'd never apologize, of course. At least he'd go

away. I let out a breath in relief and tied my robe shut.

[MarieSclavo: Gates is here. Sending him in.]

The door opened. I smiled and leaned against the doorway to my office. Senator Gates thanked Marie as he slipped inside. His gaze snapped to me and he ignored everything else. Marie shut the door.

"Thank you for coming, Senator." I sashayed across the office to him. At the same time, I issued a command to the security AI to lock my office door.

"I'm always happy to hear how I can help Godhand International." He tossed his raincoat to the side and set his hands on my hips.

Gates wore a dark suit rumpled from a long day of dealing with lobbyists and other politicians. Once upon a time, he'd been an athlete, serving on a crew team. Now in his fifties, his muscle had faded with disuse and his gut had grown a small paunch. His graying dark hair had remained thick and wavy, at least.

This man chaired the committee overseeing West America's business entanglements, including the government's interest in the Borders and Enclaves Board. Without his committee's approval, it didn't matter how well I wooed Mr. Figueroa. The government could rule against us, and that would be the end of our bid for extraterritoriality. Gates in particular wouldn't rule against me, but he needed convincing to cajole the rest of the committee to line up behind him. I hadn't bothered to broach the subject before now because I hadn't had an in with Mr. Figueroa.

I slipped my hands under his suit jacket and eased it off his shoulders. He sighed with contentment. Brushing my nose against his, I loosened his tie.

"You must've had a hard day, Senator."

"The budget is due in two weeks. Everyone is scrambling to make the numbers work." His breath smelled of his usual coffee and mint.

"That must be exhausting, and you must be famished." With both ends of his tie in my hands, I urged him to an armchair. A covered platter sat on the coffee table and an open bottle of champagne chilled in a cooler sleeve.

"Yes, on both counts. Every year, we all swear we'll get the budget done sooner, and every year, we all delay for one thing or another." He slumped in the chair and poured himself champagne.

I knelt between his legs. Not because he wanted a blow job. He didn't. Because he wanted someone to make him feel powerful and in control. "No one really understands how hard you work for your country."

"No, they don't."

Picking up the platter, I removed the lid to show him the contents. He nodded. I set the platter on his lap so he could take what he wanted. Me choosing and feeding him defeated the point. Instead, he picked up a cracker covered in salmon pâté and pushed it into my mouth. He enjoyed feeding me more than himself—deciding what, when, how, and how much I ate fulfilled his desire for control.

"And what do you want from me today?" he asked while I licked caviar off his finger.

Once upon a time, I played coy with him, trying to make it seem less like a transaction and more like a relationship. I knew better now. He wanted a supplicant, and he wanted to set the price. "We're applying to the B&E Board."

"Ah. Yes." He scooped another fingerful of caviar and slipped it into my mouth. "I had a feeling that would come soon. Godhand is becoming a big league player. I'm not sure if you're really ready yet, though."

"We have offices in eight countries and manufacturing in four."

He chuckled and kept feeding me. "West America,

Canada, and the United States only count as three separate countries in the most technical sense. We're entangled with both."

"But not subservient."

"True. Still." He picked up the last bite of brie on a cracker and ate it. "You're not exactly on par with the other companies on the board." He brushed the tip of a strawberry across my lips.

Playing my part, I whimpered at the temptation without trying to eat it. "The West American Army rated our internal security force Triple-A. Our market cap is now five billion. And we employ over thirty-thousand of your constituents. We might not be BezOhben yet, but we'll get there within a few years, and extraterritoriality will help us. Besides, we'll still pay taxes without getting police protection at our six West America facilities. We'll save those regions a lot of money. And that will help your budgets."

He pushed the strawberry into my mouth. I offered a flicker of resistance, enough for him to feel it. As I bit down on the red flesh close enough to brush my lips over his thumb and finger, he shivered. "Take off the robe."

Like an obedient dog, I untied the sash and let my robe slide off my shoulders. "What else do you want,

Senator?"

"Stand up." He popped a bite of cheesecake into his mouth while I followed orders. "Let your hair loose."

I tugged out the clips holding my hair in place. Thick waves of silvery blonde hair slipped to my shoulders.

For several long moments, he stared at me, drinking in the sight. I shook out my hair, putting on a show for him.

"Go—" His voice cracked. He set the tray aside and I saw the bulge in his pants. I had a feeling tonight would be light on foreplay. "Go stand at the foot of the bed with your back to the door."

"Yes, Senator." I did as I was told.

Cloth rustled, telling me that he removed some clothing, probably his shirt. He followed me into the bedroom and pressed his body against my back. His hands touched my hips and his breath warmed my chest. My skin crawled, but I ignored it.

"How much do you want extraterritoriality?"

I moaned for him. He had a script he followed, and I knew what to say. "I want it, Senator."

"Beg," he whispered.

"Please. I'll do anything for it, Senator."

"Anything?"

"Anything at all. Please, Senator. Make me pay."

Some days, my job made me a whore. I'd learned to live with that.

# CHAPTER 4

[MarieSclavo: Ross wants a meeting. Are you dressed yet?]

I stood at my desk, checking weekly reports from my department heads, something I did every Thursday morning at nine. Before he left around midnight, Gates had promised to secure the votes for me. One more man down, one still to go. With luck, I'd have the whole thing wrapped by next weekend, and could move on to my next plan.

[VictoriaGodhand: Yes, you can let him in.]

Ross strolled in, crisp and fresh in a dark gray suit. His possessive smile spoke volumes. Especially when his eyes lingered on my ass.

"How did your meeting with Gates go?"

"Good morning to you too."

One corner of his mouth twitched like he found me amusing. He stopped a few feet away and tucked his hands into the pockets of his slacks. "Good morning, Vickie."

"It went fine, thank you." And now, we danced. He wanted something, and I wanted him not to have it. Whatever "it" was.

"The AI didn't record what time he left."

"It probably didn't record what time he arrived, either."

"So when did he leave?"

"As soon as our meeting concluded. Which shouldn't surprise you."

Ross frowned at me. "Why are you being cagey about it?"

"Why do you care?"

"I just worry about you."

Glancing at him, I couldn't tell how he meant that. "I can take care of myself."

"You shouldn't have to."

"I don't have to. This is my job, not my sainted calling. If I decide I don't like it, I can walk away anytime." I wished he'd walk away—from me, from the company, from the country.

He huffed and stepped closer to take my hand. "That's not what I meant. You could lean on me. Let me do some of the heavy lifting."

"I'm fine." I tugged my hand free.

"Vickie, you hardly ever leave the building. You're overworked. Let me take you away for a few days. We'll sit on a beach and relax."

I kept myself from laughing in his face by the skin of my teeth. As if a vacation with him would be relaxing. A trip with Marie sounded nice, though. "This is a very bad time for me to take a break from work. I have several projects in progress, and all of them have sensitive timetables."

"What projects? Maybe I can shift some staff to get you extra help."

Raising an eyebrow, I tried to imagine his angle. Did he want to undermine my authority in the company? He wouldn't get far trying to do that in private. "Ross, knock it off. I have enough staff and I'm fine. If you have some complaint about my job performance, take it up with my father."

He raised his hands in surrender. "I only want to help."

Of course he did. Help himself, though, not me. I raised an eyebrow. "In what way is distracting me so I can't do my job helpful?"

Stepping back, he shook his head. "Message received. Vickie is working. Save it for dinner. Wear something nice? I'll make sure you're waited on by people who know how to pamper."

I waved him off and stopped paying attention to him. If he behaved himself tonight, I'd call it a victory. While handling department issues, I considered what to wear tonight. Ross didn't deserve a new dress, so I'd have Marie pick something from my closet.

The rest of my day passed in the usual blur of getting things done. Prepping for incoming hostile employees always took time and effort. The nerds of BowerTech would resist at first, then they'd see the wisdom of joining GIInc. A shiny new lab with better tools would speed the process. I had to identify what they'd want, clear space for it, order it, and have it set up. Short-term housing also needed arranging.

A few minutes after four in the afternoon, Marie passed through my office without a word. I joined her in my closet. She picked a silver dress that hit me at the knees and covered both my chest and shoulders. Ross didn't need the encouragement of bare skin to touch me.

We added silver wires hanging over my ears to dangle crushed diamonds from my lobes, a black choker with more crushed diamonds, two silver bangle bracelets, and black sticks to hold my hair in a bun. Silver heels and the makeup printer completed the look.

Marie stepped back to survey our handiwork. "You look too nice for Ross."

"But not nice enough for you."

She sighed. "You could still call this off."

"I could. He'd ask a lot of questions, and then still keep hitting on me. It's better if I just find out what he really wants and tell him why he can't have it." I checked the clock in my visual overlay—4:37. Ross had a penchant for showing up inconveniently early, so he'd arrive soon. "Have something decadent for dinner. Use my account to pay."

Marie kissed my cheek. "Don't let him get away with too much."

With a walk across my bedroom in heels higher than I usually wore, I found my balance. Even if I couldn't walk fast, I could stab Ross with a heel at need.

[RossLynch: Are you ready to go?]

[VictoriaGodhand: Almost.] I could've said yes, but didn't out of nothing more than pique.

[RossLynch: I'm on my way there.]

Great. He wouldn't stop outside my office, so he'd

see Marie. Rather than waiting for him to message me again or walk into my office, I opened the door and stepped out. Halfway down the hall, he saw me and smiled. Darkness and greed flickered in his expression before he tamped them down. My guard raised. Verbal sparring might not cover all my bases tonight.

"You're beautiful, as always."

Thanks, Ross, for saying the effort I put in made no difference. The statement might also have meant more if he hadn't stared at my breasts while delivering it. "Thank you."

He offered his arm. "Would you like to go someplace you know, or someplace you don't?"

"SkyCity." When entertaining the enemy, a familiar place seemed best. If Ross tried anything, the waitstaff would come to my aid. As a bonus, they served the best salmon in town.

"As the lady commands."

We used the dedicated limo perch. He opened the door and slid in beside me. The long, black car slid out of the building under his command. I watched the skyline through the window. For once, rain didn't obscure the view. The sun slipped through patchy clouds toward the mountains, painting the sky with darkening orange.

He settled his hand on my thigh. I ignored it. Or rather, I tried to. Many men had done much worse. Despite that, his touch always left me feeling grimy. No one else caused that. I crossed my legs and batted at his hand.

Ross crossed his arms. "What's the matter?"

"Nothing."

"We're supposed to be having a pleasant night out together."

"I'm not in the mood." Glancing aside, I saw his brow furrowing.

"Were you in the mood for Senator Gates?" He seemed to try to hide a scowl.

"What's that supposed to mean? Are you sulking because I didn't introduce you to him?"

"I'm not sulking," he snapped. "I'm asking if you slept with him."

I snorted. "No." No sleeping whatsoever had taken place with Senator Gates. Even if it had, I could lie to Ross's face any day of the week.

"Then why won't you tell me when he left?"

I dismissed him with a flick of my hand. "You shouldn't even know he was there. The more people who know about meetings like that, the more chance it gets flagged as corruption and the company loses our influence on the Corporate Oversight Committee. The Attorney General would love to use someone like Dave Gates as an example to scare all the politicians straight."

Ross stewed. I could feel it in the air. He said nothing else until we reached the Space Needle and its revolving restaurant at the top. Since he hadn't bothered to call ahead, we had to wait five minutes while they prepped my father's favorite table for us. We sat on one side of a table with me next to a huge window overlooking the orange glow of sunset as it played across the city. Though our chairs offered no barriers between us and he scooted close, he kept his hands to himself. The boy could learn.

I logged into the local system to place my order, as I'd done on a thousand previous visits.

[SkyCityAtTheSpaceNeedle: Your table's ticket is already closed. Thank you for accessing our node. Your order has been entered into the kitchen queue and will be served as soon as it's ready.]

Squinting at Ross, wishing I could crack his head open and see what made him tick, I asked, "Did you order for me?"

"Yes."

My favorite waiter, Tom, brought a bottle of champagne and poured for us. He seemed to sense tension at the table. Aside from flashing me a polite, friendly smile, he said nothing and slipped out of sight as soon as he had filled both flutes.

"Why champagne?" I asked.

"Why not?"

"Cancel whatever you ordered for me."

Ross raised an eyebrow. "Why? You always get the same thing. I was just saving time."

"I do not."

"Yes, you do. Parmesan-crusted salmon with rice pilaf and mixed vegetables."

Admittedly, I did get that dish often. "That's not the only thing I order here."

"No." Ross huffed. "But you get that nine times out of ten."

The authority with which he said that made me wonder if he'd been checking up on me. Granted, he came to dinner with us three or four times a week, but he seemed to sure of himself. I stifled a grimace.

"Cancel it. I can order for myself."

"Fine."

As soon as the system opened the ticket, I ordered the parmesan-crusted salmon with rice pilaf and mixed vegetables. It still sounded good, and I had a whole evening's worth of pique to use up.

I sipped my champagne and watched the sun setting on the Sound. Marie liked the view from here. She seldom got to see it. The last time I brought her, we'd come with my dad and Viola on Secretaries' Day for lunch. I remembered the way the water sparkled and how it had matched Marie's eyes.

"Why are we here?"

"Because you like it." Ross chugged his entire glass and poured more for himself. He replaced the bottle without asking if I wanted more.

"Why are we having dinner?"

"That's a thing normal people do after work."

If he wanted to play snarky and difficult, so could I. "What makes you think I'm normal?"

"Victoria," he chided, using exactly the same tone as my father.

I stood. He grabbed my arm.

"Where are you going?"

"Home. Enjoy your food. And mine."

"Sit down," he growled.

Unimpressed, I yanked my arm. He didn't let go.

I bent to put my mouth next to his ear. "Let go or I'm going to scream," I whispered.

He let go and smacked a small black box on the table. "Jesus Christ, Vickie. You can't even sit and have dinner with me? To think I brought you here to fucking propose."

For several beats, I stared at the box, too stunned to react. He'd asked me out to propose. Marriage. To me. Never had I given him any positive signals. We hadn't dated at any point. Every time he'd asked me to do something in the past, I'd declined. All his groping in the elevator had earned him nothing. The first time he took me to a restaurant without Dad, he thought I'd gush and accept?

I laughed. At first, he flinched, then I saw anger build up in his shoulders and brow.

"You're terrible at this," I told him through giggles.

The waiter brought our orders. Ross watched Tom set the plates down. He glowered at mine.

"You ordered the same fucking thing?"

"Tom, could you box mine, please?" I grinned, watching Ross's anger blossom into rage.

Ross vibrated but did nothing.

Tom picked up my plate and fled.

"Oh, Ross, you poor thing." I patted his shoulder, moving my hand to get him three times despite his shrugging away. Leaning to reach his ear again, I whispered, "I'm already seeing someone, and you're not even close to what I want in a partner."

Tom reappeared and handed me a box. "Have a nice evening, Miss Godhand."

"Thank you, Tom. See you next time." Pleased with myself, I turned my back on Ross and walked away. I didn't care whose account they billed. Either Ross would pay for it, or they'd put it on my dad's tab.

# CHAPTER 5

The next morning, I sat around a coffee table with the rest of the executives to deliver weekly reports. Despite my best efforts, no other women had joined the upper ranks of our executive team. When I took over, that would change. All ten men wore suits in the same three shades of navy and gray, and half had gray hair like Dad. The rest varied in age, but not complexion or general appearance.

For some reason, Ross led the meeting with Dad overseeing in thoughtful silence. No one seemed to find that strange, though we'd all learned long ago to roll with change. So long as Dad stayed calm, there could be a dead body on the table and no one would give it more than a curious glance.

My input included the minor items the team had come to expect from me. Few members of the team knew much about my job, and I preferred to keep that true. If they all believed I pulled a bloated salary for over-glorified secretary work, so much the better. I preferred being underestimated any day of the week. Plausible deniability also worked in my favor.

"That covers me," I said, having finished my report. "Caleb?" I looked to the VP sitting next to me.

"Just a moment, Caleb." Ross smiled at me, pleasant like a viper. "Victoria, I think we'd all like to hear a little more about the BowerTech deal."

I stared at him, blinking. My report hadn't mentioned BowerTech, and he had no way to know I'd initiated an op against them. Budgeting for the new lab hadn't yet exceeded my usual division expenses, so unless he saw something specific with his own eyes, he had no way to know about it.

"I'm not aware of a BowerTech deal. As I reported two weeks ago, they rejected our second offer."

He watched me so intently that I wondered if he'd gone digging through my files just to try to embarrass me this morning. "I thought you were preparing a third offer."

"Then you weren't paying attention," I said, getting annoyed with him. "As I noted at the time, raising the offer isn't cost-effective."

"I remember that," Caleb said with a nod. "We discussed some in-house options and ultimately rejected them all. The sector isn't profitable enough. Space-based solar solutions—"

"We don't need to rehash that discussion," another VP grumbled. "Move on."

"Of course. Go ahead, Caleb." Ross kept watching me. Had he thought I'd crack and spill about my BowerTech op? His nods to the other VPs told me he kept paying attention as the others spoke, but his gaze stuck with me the whole time.

I spent the next half hour stifling the urge to squirm. The meeting ended on time, as it always did. Everyone stood and left to tend to their other duties, except Ross, Dad, and me. I stayed in my spot, letting the other execs filter around me. The last man out shut the door.

"What the fuck was that?" I snapped at Ross.

"Go fuck yourself," Ross spat.

"Children." Dad paced to his desk and picked up a tablet. "Is there a problem?"

"She humiliated me in public last night!"

"You humiliated yourself by being a moron," I said.

"Let's not have name calling," Dad said. He tapped

on his tablet, showing where his attention lay. "This is a place of business, not a schoolyard."

Ross seethed with rage. I saw it in his eyes, shoulders, and fists. "I asked her to marry me and she said no."

"Victoria," Dad said, using that tone.

"Victoria what? Of course I said no!"

Ross crossed his arms and lifted his chin to look down his nose at me.

Dad raised an eyebrow. "We discussed this."

"In what version of reality does me saying 'I'll take it under advisement' get translated to 'yes, Daddy, whatever you say'? I'm not some fucking door prize for him because he managed to claw his way up the corporate ladder."

"She didn't just laugh in my face in SkyCity, loud enough for the whole restaurant to hear, she lied about having a boyfriend already."

Dad looked up from his tablet with a frown. "You're seeing someone?"

While I didn't strictly need to protect Marie from my dad, I had no intention of telling Ross. "Yes."

"When were you planning on introducing me?"

"When I'm sure it makes sense to do so."

"Ah. It's not serious. You should let Ross try to win

you over."

"Yes," Ross said with an excessive amount of smugness, "you should."

Several angry responses bubbled in my head. I snapped my mouth shut to keep them inside. Suggesting Ross cut off his dick to appeal to me wouldn't have improved the situation. "No, thank you," I said through clenched teeth.

Dad sighed as he sat in the chair behind his desk. "Toria, you need to consider the company."

"Excuse me? I've given this company everything I am for the past sixteen years. I worked for you while I was still in high school and all the way through college. I've sacrificed everything for you and this company, and you have the gall to lecture me about being selfish?" I shook my head and turned my back on him, intending to leave.

"That's exactly what I'm talking about," Dad said.

I stopped with my hand on the doorknob. "What?"

"Ross, leave us. This is between me and my daughter, not the CEO, COO, and a VP."

Ross scowled and let his arms fall to his sides, but he left without another word. I opened the door for him and restrained myself from smacking him in the ass with it. Once I'd closed it, I still wanted to murder someone. My father deciding to make the conversation private hadn't taken away my anger over the subject.

Dad sighed as I approached his desk. "Toria, I love you very much. I'm sure I do a lousy job of showing it, but you're the most important thing in the world to me."

I sat in the chair opposite him, not sure where this conversation would go. He'd already blunted my anger. "I love you too, Dad. You're not dying of some horrible disease, are you?"

He smiled. "No. I'm in good shape. It's you I'm worried about. When was the last time you left the building?"

"Yesterday. I sat in a restaurant with Ross for fifteen minutes. We had champagne. I laughed. He didn't."

With a huff, he fixed me with a bemused yet stern glare. "For something other than work or a meal with a fellow executive?"

That question stumped me. For a few moments, I considered lying, but didn't see a reason. "I don't remember."

"That's what I'm talking about. You don't have a life, Toria. You live and breathe the company. You haven't taken a single vacation day. Ever. I checked. In sixteen years, you've missed exactly three days of work. One for your high school graduation, one for your college graduation, and one for your mother's funeral. On top of that, I'm willing to bet you put in hours on the weekends that don't get logged."

Put in stark terms like that, I had to admit it sounded like a nightmarish, grinding march. "You don't exactly skip out all the time."

He raised his brow. "I take at least three weeks of vacation every year, including the one I'm leaving for tonight, and I was out for a month when Amelie passed."

"Fine." I still didn't know what he wanted. "What's your actual point?"

"Who's this man you're seeing?"

"None of your business."

"Because he's imaginary?"

"No."

He reached under his desk and flipped the privacy switch. My implant informed me it had lost its connection. I pursed my lips, still not sure I wanted him to know. I'd been protecting Marie for so long that revealing her felt wrong, like a betrayal.

"If you can't tell me now, I'm going to have to assume he's a fiction you insist upon clinging to for some reason. Which sounds like a reason to see a psychologist. Have you been 'seeing' him since your mother passed?"

Rolling my eyes, I huffed in annoyance. "I'm not seeing a man."

"There. Now we can talk about Ross."

"No. Because I'm seeing a woman."

Dad stared at me, blinking. He opened his mouth, then shut it without saying anything. I'd never seen him so confused. "Say that again?"

"I'm dating a woman, Dad. I'm not interested in Ross because I'm not interested in men." Of course, him being an asshole had something to do with it too. If Dad had picked a sweet, charming man, I might've taken one for the team.

"Why the hell didn't you say something sooner? All this time, I've been expecting grandkids at some point. I could've done...something. I don't know what, but something."

I sighed. All this angst had been about babies. "She's younger than me and wants to have a baby. We just have to go to one of those labs. You'll get your grandkids. All this is waiting for the B&E Board deal to go through. That damned application has eaten my life for the past two years. I don't have any other major projects on my current timeline, so once that's done, I should be able to handle it."

"Well. Okay. That's...good." Dad never lost his cool, so I knew I'd blindsided him. Since I saw him every day, that meant I'd hidden Marie well. "Who is she?"

If I couldn't tell him now, I couldn't tell him at all. We had to get married before any lab would do the ova-blending procedure anyway. He deserved to be there for the wedding. "Marie. She knows all my dirty secrets and loves me anyway."

He stared and seemed at a loss for words.

"I know it's cliché to fall for your secretary." I grinned. "I didn't do it on purpose."

Dad chuckled. "Yes, it is." He rubbed his face like the whole world had turned upside down. "In case you're curious, I've never had an affair with Viola."

"I don't care, Dad. Fuck whoever you want. Fuck Ross for all I care."

His grimace told me he'd begun to process my unexpected news. "No, thank you. You should bring Marie to the dinner party tomorrow night."

"No. I'm worried about people using her against me. As soon as our B&E bid is concluded successfully, I'm going to pull a new secretary from the pool and have Marie train her, then she'll get laid off." I smirked. "With a nice severance package."

"I see." Dad grinned, so I knew he didn't mind. "Why am I not surprised you have this planned well in advance?"

"Because you know how I work."

He nodded and sobered. "Thank you for telling me. I wish you'd brought it up sooner, but I think I understand why you didn't.

The meeting felt done. I reached out and touched his hand. "Thank you for listening."

# CHAPTER 6

"You look amazing." Marie stepped back from her handiwork and set the makeup printer on shelf.

I checked myself in the floor-length mirror on the back of our closet door and agreed with her. She'd piled my hair on top of my head in an elegant confection dripping with sapphires. Deep, dark blue silk in delicate folds draped over my body to the floor with my neck and shoulders bare. Sapphires hung from a silver chain around my neck.

Later, when the formal evening of forced politeness ended, I'd come home and she'd undo all her careful work.

Marie sighed. "The worst part is how I want to touch you, but I can't because it'll mess up everything."

Wanting to savor that look on her face forever, I issued a command for my implant to take a picture of her.

[VictoriaGodhandSystem: Image storage 98% full.]

My to-do list gained an item—sort through my saved

images and download the ones I didn't want in my head anymore.

Her face fell. "Ross is here to pick you up."

Weeks ago, Dad had arranged for Ross to escort me in his stead. Before he left yesterday evening, he'd reminded me to play nice without the usual admonition to try dating him. That moment had been refreshing. I still lamented keeping Marie a secret from him for so long.

"Sooner I leave, sooner I return." I took her hand and kissed the back. We walked to my office together. "Don't wait up. I'll wake you when I get back."

"Don't cause too much trouble." She waved from the bedroom door.

The hem of my dressed kicked out with every step in my two-inch heels. I met Ross at the limo landing pad. He looked good in his tux, with his precisely arranged hair. Every movement he made seemed stiff, suggesting Dad might've told him to back off. Finally.

We remained quiet until Ross asked if I knew who we'd see at the party. The question seemed innocent enough. I offered the list and we chatted about which targets deserved priority. With Dad, I would've had a similar conversation. My evening had a basic script and a loose schedule. But I'd done this a thousand times, and none of it mattered much. These parties provided nothing more than ordinary networking.

Our host's home not only cut off access to the WAINet, it boasted AR overlays for every wall, window, and fixture, allowing his guests to select from multiple themes for our own visual and aural enjoyment. Bots rolled around three rooms and a patio carrying trays full of sparkling wine, designer narcotics, and finger foods. With our evening attire, we fit in among the guests, who ranged from my age to borderline-decrepit.

I kissed cheeks, laughed at horrible jokes, and ignored men patting my ass. Ross and I split up and mingled separately. Thank goodness. He could've clung to my arm, but instead circulated like an adult.

After finishing a glass of wine, I excused myself to the bathroom I'd used at a dozen or so previous parties. On my way out of the bathroom, I ran into someone in the wood-paneled hall separating us from the party. The lights had been turned off, and I saw only his silhouette, but I smelled Ross's cologne. I shrank against the wall to shuffle past. He blocked me with his body and wrapped an arm around me.

"Who is he, Vickie?" he purred into my ear. Alcohol

had turned his breath sour.

"None of your business." I wriggled to escape his grasp. He held on tighter.

He licked my ear. "You're mine."

In the past, he'd groped my ass and brushed his chest against mine. He'd come close to nibbling on my ear once. On several occasions, I'd suffered through him kissing my hand. Never had he licked any portion of my body.

I shied away from him. "That only works for desserts."

"You're my dessert." He shoved me against the wall.

Fear flared in my belly. I met his gaze and saw restrained violence. "Back off—" My voice cracked. Shoving against him did me no good. He resisted my efforts without trying.

He pressed his mouth to mine and proved both that he didn't know a damned thing about kissing and he'd had too much to drink already. I turned my head. His hand flew so fast I didn't see it coming when he slapped me. Pain exploded across my cheek. Then he muffled my scream by shoving his hand over my mouth.

"What's his name? I swear, if you scream when I take my hand away, I will beat you so fucking hard you'll have to

DARKSIDE SEATTLE: FIXER

go to the emergency room."

Sparks of panic jolted through my body to my fingers and toes. With alcohol keeping him from controlling himself, I believed him when he said he'd beat the shit out of me.

Another guest stumbled into the hallway, her heels giving her trouble in the dark. She giggled. Ross hustled me through a door as the lights flickered on, his grip too strong for me to overcome. He'd found a guest bedroom, the last place I want to wind up alone with an enraged man of any kind. I wanted to be here with Ross even less.

My heels betrayed me. I fell to the floor between the door and the bed. Ross pounced on me. Lying on my back, I tried to push him off. He grabbed my wrists and pinned my arms over my head.

With his nose an inch from mine, he growled, "What the fuck is his name?" His eyes flashed with rage. His bitter breath choked me.

I flinched away and squeezed my eyes shut. Helpless against him, I prayed for someone to stumble across us.

"God, you're beautiful tonight."

Fuck. From what I knew of him, I could guess he got off on control, like Senator Gates. His thoughts had, perhaps inevitably, wandered to sex. While I could handle sex with men, I didn't enjoy it much. His fresh intent, of forcing it on me, churned my stomach with terror.

I thrashed. I rolled. I wriggled. I kicked.

In the middle of it, he hit me in the gut. I threw up, spraying bile and half-digested wine into his face. He squawked and rolled off me, swiping his jacket sleeve across his face. Sparking with raw, fear-fueled anger, my mouth dripping with disgusting acid, and tears streaming down my cheeks, I planted my knee between his legs and scrambled to get away.

He flailed and wailed, curling around his crotch. Despite his distress, he snared my ankle. I kicked. He howled and clutched his wrist. All I cared about was that he let go. Lurching to my feet, I gasped for breath.

Ross moaned in a ball. I spat at him and kicked him in the shin. He whimpered. With him on the floor, defeated, I straightened and looked down my nose at him.

"I'm a lesbian, you asshat. There is no 'he.' " With that, I stormed out and avoided the party on my way to the front door. My implant reconnected to the WAINet. The limo came at my call. I held everything together until I climbed in, shut the door, and entered my preferred destination.

Hugging myself in the leather seat, I broke down and cried. My whole body shook. Nothing made sense. Ross hadn't done much, but I still felt scared and violated. Despite knowing I flew over the city at two hundred feet, part of me expected Ross to rip the limo door open and attack.

The limo landed too soon and not soon enough. My eyes blurry from tears, I stared at the door. Somehow, my mind whispered, Ross had beaten me here. Any moment, he'd rip the door open. But I needed to get out of this dress. I couldn't breathe in it.

Smacking the release, I stumbled out and wobbled to the elevator. The doors opened too fast and not fast enough. How had I not lost a shoe? The fucking things kept me from running. I wanted to rip them off my feet, but I wanted to reach my bedroom more. At least no one saw me.

I reached my office door and locked it behind me.

"You're awfully ear—" Marie stepped into the doorway wearing a lavender teddy I'd given her for her birthday. She covered her mouth and sucked in a breath. "What happened?" When I shook my head, she rushed forward and put her arms around me. "Never mind. Come here and let's clean you up."

Trying to stop weeping, I let her guide me. I sat where

she wanted and covered my face. Her soft, deft hands removed everything holding my hair together. As she worked, she made soothing noises and let me cry. She pulled my shoes off.

"Tori, are you bleeding?"

I opened my eyes. She held up my shoe with blood spattered on the heel and bottom. Sniffling and shaking my head, I wondered if I'd killed Ross. He could've bled to death on that floor. How did I feel about that? No idea. It swirled into everything else.

When I didn't answer because I could only stare, she helped me out of my dress and wrapped me in a soft, fluffy robe. She tucked me into bed and snuggled with me. After a while, I stopped crying. I felt like I'd been wrung out. Marie kept me warm. Without her, I knew I'd be empty and hollow.

"Ross attacked me at the party," I finally said in the dim, flickering light of a fake fire Marie had set up on the screen across from the bed.

"Attacked you?"

"He was drunk."

Marie squeezed me. "And you stabbed him with your shoe. Because you're incredible." She kissed my neck.

"Amazing."

She chased away the last of my chills and reminded me why I loved her.

# CHAPTER 7

Marie groaned, waking me on Sunday morning. "Too early," she grumbled.

"For what?" I kept my eyes closed and brushed my nose against Marie's neck. I spooned her, my arms wrapped around her. Her fierce warmth blazed against my bare skin.

"For Jay. He's got your trains. Wants to know when to meet."

I cracked an eye open to check the time in my visual display—8:34am. We'd slept in. "After lunch. Call it one in the afternoon. Get a message to Figueroa's office to set up a meeting for me as soon as possible. I'll get breakfast." Slipping out of the covers, I found my robe in a pile on the floor.

With a sigh, Marie rolled onto her back and watched me slip into the robe. "How long after the meeting with Figueroa until the B&E project is done?"

"Depends on the speed of the votes. Could be a day, could be a month. I wouldn't expect longer than that, though. My guess is by Friday."

"I'll have my replacement come in tomorrow so he can get the hang of the job."

"You don't want to run some interviews or anything?"

Marie waved me off. "I hired someone three months ago. He's been handling secondary matters and is already up to speed on Jay. I'll spend a day or two helping him find the groove, then I'm going to lounge about and eat bonbons until you're ready to get me knocked up."

I laughed as I crossed the room to our small kitchen to fetch pastries and juice.

"Jay confirms he'll be there." She batted her eyelashes at me as I brought a plate to bed. "Whatever shall we do until you have to go?"

"We can probably think of something." I swiped my finger through sweetened cream cheese on a danish and smeared it across her lips. She licked my finger. "Thank you for last night. I think I can face Ross tomorrow, and that's because of you."

"Maybe you should leave the blood on your shoe and

wear those heels."

"I love you, woman."

Hours later, I landed my car next to Jay's nondescript gray sedan with the jammer active. He hopped out of his car with a brown paper bag and slid into the passenger seat of mine.

Flashing me a brilliant grin, he handed me a paper bag. "Model is handmade and functional, chocolate is Swiss. As promised. Your BowerTech op is set to run tomorrow night. I've got a location to stash the meat assets until you're ready to transfer them. The tech assets will be delivered Tuesday morning. Preliminary estimate says it'll take four vans. Which facility do you want them sent to?"

"Seatac. Prep to move the meat on Thursday. That'll give a full day to arrange the lab with the acquired tech before they're brought in. You have my permission to tap one if needed to keep the others in line." By the time Dad returned from his trip, the whole BowerTech situation would be taken care of.

"Yes, ma'am. I'll make sure the operatives know that. You need anything else?"

I thought about asking him for a quote on hitting Ross. Dad liked him, though. If I could poison that, I didn't need Ross to die. Besides, I could live with avoiding otherwise empty rooms with him. I'd tell Dad that I couldn't work parties with him, so that situation would never happen again.

"Plan to take a vacation after the BowerTech op," I said. "Because I'm going to. At least a week, maybe two. Probably take me another week to ramp into a new project."

"Yes, ma'am. I'll lie low. Maybe hit the beach for part of it." He grinned. "It's awful this time of year, so no one'll think to look for me there. There's a few new contacts I'd like to cultivate, too."

"Thanks, Jay."

"My bank account thanks you in return. Take care of yourself and good luck with the train thing." He slipped out and shut the door.

I went home. By some bizarre miracle, no disasters or messages from Ross interrupted me from enjoying the rest of the day. Marie and I went out to dinner as boss and secretary, then I let her drag me along while she shopped for a cute dress to get married in. I expected to marry her at the courthouse over lunch on a weekday, so I didn't think she needed special clothes, but I didn't mind buying her a pretty dress.

# CHAPTER 8

Monday morning came with my Dad on vacation and Ross filling in for him. Instead of me. Because I had other things to worry about, or some crap like that. Regardless, bright and early, as Marie straightened my suit jacket for me, I got a message from Ross.

[RossLynch: Would you please come to the CEO office at your earliest convenience?]

"What's wrong?" Marie asked.

"I didn't think I let that show."

"Not much." She traced my eyebrow and let her finger trail past my eye. "I see it here."

"Hmph." I didn't like being easy to read, but maybe only Marie could see it.

"So, what's wrong?"

I sighed. She didn't need to worry. "Ross wants to chat."

[VictoriaGodhand: I'll be there in a few minutes.]

Marie's eyes narrowed. "Tell him to go to hell."

Smiling at my beloved defender, I kissed the tip of her nose. "I'll be back soon. To do work. Because it's Monday." I left without giving her a chance to distract me. When I returned, she'd be in her work clothes and work persona, giving away nothing but the ordinary devotion of an employee loyal to her employer. The day she never had to force herself into that box again would be a good day.

I nodded to Viola on my way into Dad's office. Ross sat in my father's chair, tapping on my father's tablet at my father's desk. He looked comfortable. Too comfortable. I almost wondered if he wore one of my father's suits, but Ross had broader shoulders and two inches of height on Dad. He'd probably taken socks and underwear.

Ross raised his head to watch me approach the desk, his expression inscrutable. I stopped a few feet away and crossed my arms. A skin-tone bandage poked out of his shirt cuff. Otherwise, he seemed fine.

We stared at each other for several seconds. With every fleck of my will, I wanted him to cave.

He cleared his throat and broke eye contact to flick his gaze to my chest. "Malcolm asked me oversee things in his absence. Did you have anything you wanted to report?"

Apparently, we would pretend nothing had happened. I considered whether to play along or not. Dad slotting Ross into Acting CEO chafed. Technically, Ross had the power to fire me. Not that the Board of Directors would allow him to when I owned one third of the company's stock and Dad owned another third, but he could shut me out for a day or two. "No."

"Are you sure?" He reached under the desk, probably groping for the jammer switch. I did not want to ever again wind up alone with Ross in a room without a WAINet connection. "He said you're usually busy enough over the weekend to have a report on Monday mornings."

"You were at the party, you saw how early I left. And I decided to take a day to myself yesterday. Which shouldn't shock anyone, as it was Sunday."

"Ah. Yes. The party." He leaned back in the chair without activating the jammer, getting much too comfortable in the fine leather. "I don't remember much about what happened." Something about the way he watched me made me wonder how much he did remember. Probably more than he wanted me to believe. "I seem to have had a little more wine and less food than I should have. Dinner on the way would have been prudent. For both of us."

I didn't want to discuss it. When Dad returned, I'd chat with him about it. Bothering him during his vacation with something distressing seemed wrong. He needed that annual trip to unpack his memories of Mom.

"Did you want anything else?"

Ross stood and buttoned his jacket. He smiled at me, and it felt predatory. At least he hadn't turned on the jammer. With his arm out to embrace me, he approached. I thought about punching him in his smug face. Instead, I turned to head for the door. He closed the distance faster than I expected and put his arm around my waist.

"I think we've had some misunderstandings. Have lunch with me. We should chat outside of the office."

[MarieSclavo: Meeting with Figueroa is set for two this afternoon.]

[VictoriaGodhand: Good.]

I flashed Ross a fake smile. "I already have plans."

"Are we back to that old routine?" Ross sighed. His hand slid to my ass.

Disgusted by him, I stiffened. Before I could pull away, he shoved me forward and pinned me to the door from behind.

DARKSIDE SEATTLE: FIXER

"Get off me or I'm calling the cops," I growled.

He let go and backed off, holding up his hands in surrender. "I can't control myself when you wear skirts like that."

Glaring at him, I yanked the door open. "Try," I spat. I stormed out and slammed the door shut.

The short walk to my office did nothing to cool my temper. Maybe I needed to message Dad after all. I breezed past Marie and into my office, slamming that door shut too. Hitting things might've made me feel better, but I settled for the solace of mundane, boring work.

[MarieSclavo: It went well, I take it. Brad is here whenever you're ready to meet with him. We're going over workstation tasks for the moment.]

[VictoriaGodhand: That fucking sonofabitch. I'd like to murder him.]

I rubbed the back of my neck and tilted my head to stare at the ceiling. Without Marie, I thought I'd fall off the deep end.

[VictoriaGodhand: Give me about fifteen minutes, then bring him in.]

For that time, I let the mundane details of running a department threaded through the entire company distract me. Then I met my perky new secretary, a kid fresh out of college with more optimism than I ever remembered imagining, let alone having. He smiled and called me Ms. Godhand while bouncing around the office.

Watching Brad as he inspected everything bolstered my mood. He put a smile on my face. Marie and I listened while he gushed about a wide array of topics, from his favorite music to the color of his grandmother's wallpaper. Everything seemed exciting, amazing, or beautiful to him. We took him to lunch, and he loved everything about SkyCity. Provided he could settle and get the work done, I knew Marie had made a good choice.

# CHAPTER 9

Carrying my gift bag and dressed in one of my signature silver suits, I arrived fifteen minutes early for my meeting with Mr. Figueroa. His reception room had elegant decor in neutral tones, and no secretary. The B&E Board's AI checked me in and asked me to wait. The moment my butt touched the leather of a chair, the system told me to go into his office.

I walked into a large room slathered with trains. Trains of all kinds, from steam engines to the magnetic one now whisking people up and down the coast, decorated everything—AR displays, wallpaper, shelves of models, the rug, even the chairs. The desk appeared to be a scale model of a locomotive. Tracks for a model train set crossed the ceiling fifteen times.

Dominic Figueroa sat in an executive chair printed with a train scene. White streaks dominated his dark hair. A train decorated his black tie, of course. Lucia, his wife, smiled like she wanted to eat me. I returned her smile with a polite one of my own. We'd met already, as she'd been my contact to learn what Dominic wanted in the first place.

"Mr. Figueroa. Mrs. Figueroa. Thank you for seeing me on such short notice." I shut the door and crossed the room to set the gift bag on the desk.

"My pleasure," Mr. Figueroa said. "Please, Call me Dominic. I understand you've already met Lucia."

We all nodded to each other. I sat in the train-shaped chair opposite him. Lucia set a hand on the back of her husband's chair, and I noticed her fingernails—long enough to qualify as claws—had been painted in a train motif. They hadn't been like that when I met her a week ago. I wondered if Dominic made choo-choo jokes when he fucked his wife. Maybe I'd find out.

"So, Victoria." He picked up a tablet from his desk and held it for me. "I've read over Godhand's application, and I applaud you for managing to get it in front of me. My secretary sees and rejects at least twenty of these a day. The board hasn't approved one in over a year."

It had been two years and four months, but I didn't correct him.

"They're all the same," Dominic continued. "All the I's are dotted, all the T's are crossed. Every requirement is met. But we reject them all. Why do you think that is?"

"Because none of them stand out. Everyone is the same, and that's horribly boring. Besides, you're the gatekeeper for an exclusive club. You can't just give everyone a seat at the big boy table."

"Exactly."

Lucia licked her lips.

"What are you willing to do for that seat, Victoria?" Dominic picked up the bag and opened it. His face it up with delight. "Lucia, look."

Peering over his shoulder, Lucia grinned. "I told you, Mini. Her reputation is real."

"I'm prepared to offer you a relationship with Godhand International, Dominic. We won't take the seat and run like BezOhben Biotech did. They've done nothing for you since you approved their application, have they?"

"So true," Dominic said with a sigh. He handed Lucia the chocolate and set his new train model on his desk. "Such a mistake."

"Godhand won't be a mistake. I'm at your disposal any day, any time, for whatever you need."

"Whatever I need," Dominic echoed. He rolled the train model back and forth on his desk. The wheels rolled smooth and silent. "Lucia, what do I need?"

I got the feeling my day had just turned into a train kink session. So be it.

"You need someone to play Industrial Railways with you."

Dominic grinned.

I'd never heard of that before.

[VictoriaGodhandSystem: Invite to Industrial Railways received. Application is scanned and approved.]

I blinked for a moment, then couldn't help but smile. People rarely surprised me with their demands, but Dominic had blindsided me. Lucia passed me a VR headset. Accepting the invite, I slipped on the headset and relaxed into the chair. My implant interfaced with it and opened an innocent train resource game.

For two hours, I duelled Dominic in a quest to deliver the largest quantity of arcane, obsolete materials to cities that no longer existed using steam and coal-powered locomotives on metal and wood train tracks. The game failed to hold my interest, but I played anyway. All the longing looks his wife had given me must've been about the prospect of relief from playing this game for him. I imagined he pestered her about it every day.

In the end, he won by a wide margin. He beamed at me when I removed the headset. Lucia sat nearby, tapping on a tablet. She seemed happy and relaxed.

"You're good for a beginner," Dominic said. "Is there a good time for you to play, say, once a week?"

"I can make time whenever is convenient for you. I'll also check with a few employees I trust to see if anyone is familiar with the game. We should be able to get you a few people to play on a regular basis."

"That would be excellent, thank you." Such a simple thing had brought him so much joy. "I'll bring your application to the board and see it goes through. You should hear within a few days, at the most."

This seemed like a dismissal, so I stood. "Thank you, Dominic. I look forward to building the relationship between Godhand and the B&E Board." I walked out with a bounce in my step. If only all negotiations took such minimal effort.

# CHAPTER 10

Tuesday crept past with Ross leaving me alone. Marie sat in my office all day, letting Brad stay outside the door where she usually sat. As a result, I accomplished less than usual, but enjoyed my day. We had lunch in the office with Brad and sent him home for dinner. He didn't complain about anything. Dominic messaged to let me know the B&E Board had voted in our favor, and the matter had been passed to the Senate for confirmation.

Marie and I shared dinner at the small table in our suite next to the windows, watching the sun slip beneath the horizon. She'd let her dark hair loose so the thick waves brushed her shoulders. I imagined sitting with her ten, twenty, forty years from now.

She groaned and set down her fork with a clink. "I'll be back in a minute."

"What's wrong?"

Waving me off, she slipped into the office. I sighed and took another bite of herb-roasted chicken. As I chewed, she returned with her work tablet, tapping on it.

"I thought you gave that to Brad."

"Only while he's here. I'm not sure he's up to dealing with Jay's after-hours issues yet. Like now, for example." She sat and shook her head. "Problem with the op. He wants to meet as soon as you can get out to the usual spot."

My ass jumped off the chair. Jay hadn't had a "problem" in at least six months, when one of his operatives had been killed. I snatched a coat and ran for my car.

[MarieSclavo: Be careful.]

[VictoriaGodhand: Wait up for me.]

By the time I reached the car, my legs carried me at a run. I had to wait while the autoframe brought mine to the launch bay, then I had to wait while the conveyor pushed me onto the perch. More waiting drove me nuts while the car's autopilot carried me at approved speeds toward DeeSeat. Leaving the flight lane couldn't happen fast enough.

I parked the car in the dark. Jay jumped into my car. He wore ordinary jeans and a t-shirt today, with rubber boots. For the first time since I'd met him six years ago, I wondered what he did when not working for me.

"How bad is it?" I said.

"Depends on how you look at it." He scratched two days' worth of dark stubble on his cheek. "My people called off the op because they got a bad feeling."

"A bad feeling." I raised an eyebrow at him.

"Yeah. Sounds stupid, but isn't. They had a solid handle on security, then it changed tonight. Last night, everything was normal. Tonight, everything is very different. They were about to start the facility breach when they noticed extra node security and a contractor vehicle they recognized. Either we got scooped or someone ratted us. They still probed the site, but decided it looked like a grinder."

"Fuck."

"Yeah. They backed off the whole op, figuring the talent got stashed. As far as they could tell, no one saw them show up, so they set up surveillance in case the extra security pulls back. You want to set a time limit on that? It's your money."

No one knew I intended to hit BowerTech except Dad. We had no files on the subject, so even if Ross had gone through things, he wouldn't have found any information on it. Unless Dad kept notes I didn't know about outside of his implant account. Fuck, he probably did.

Something told me he had a memo program with all kinds of notes in case his shuttle crashed and I needed to take over the company. With him going on vacation to the PRC Space Station, he might've even left it in easy reach. Ross had to have gone through Dad's stuff. So he found the memos and read them, and now he knew whatever Dad had put into it about my BowerTech op.

I couldn't remember if I'd been specific about the date. Maybe Ross had only uncovered it today. And then he decided to screw it up? That didn't make sense. No matter how much he wanted me, he also wanted the company. I knew he did. That asshole had clawed and bit his way up the ladder, and he hadn't done it to win second place. No, my gut said he'd found a way to scoop BowerTech and Godhand now owned it. Unless he'd done it via death threat, he'd stolen money from someplace to pull off a third offer that the stiff-necked CEO of BowerTech hadn't been able to refuse.

In that case, he'd stepped on my job. One way or another, that asshole had done an end-run around me. Did he do it to chip away at my reputation? Did I need to consider the possibility he wanted to maneuver me out of the company? Did Dad need to worry about his position?

"Call it off. I'll authorize a partial payment for your people."

Jay flashed me a bright, fake smile. "Twenty-five percent would be polite. Thirty would make them loyal forever."

"They can have twenty. I don't want anyone spreading around that Godhand pays good if you balk."

"Can't blame me for asking. You need anything else while I'm here?"

"No." I didn't think Ross had any way to connect Jay to me, but I chose to err on the side of caution. "Take that vacation anyway. Don't go far and stay available, but get out of sight for a little bit."

"Probably a good idea. Consider me gone." He slipped out of the car.

I watched him climb into his own car, struck with an odd sort of paranoia about his safety. If Ross could hork up my op, he could kill my people. Maybe I should've spent more time running ops against Ross. We'd known him and his family for so long, I'd never considered him as an outsider who needed vetting.

For my entire ride home, I pondered the best way to ask Ross about BowerTech without him realizing I'd asked about BowerTech. The problem followed me to my office and into Marie's willing, waiting arms. The next morning, I woke with the problem still buzzing in my head. By some miracle, I hadn't dreamed about it.

By the time I went to confront Ross the next morning, I had a plan. The idea of having Marie check for a transaction regarding BowerTech occurred to me, but unless Ross had been stupid about it, there wouldn't be any paperwork yet. I barged into Dad's office and scared him enough to jump.

His whole body jerked and he swiped a tablet into his lap. "Jesus, Vickie. Fucking knock."

"Morning." My petty streak smiled. "I heard a rumor about a solar department starting, and I know Dad didn't start it because he didn't run anything past anyone. What the fuck are you up to, Ross?" In the end, I hadn't come up with anything especially brilliant. Avoiding Ross's aggravating advances for so long meant I hadn't paid enough attention to his motivations. With luck, he hadn't expected bluntness from me.

He leaned against Dad's chair as if plastered there by G-forces. "I have no idea what you're talking about."

"Don't play dumb," I snapped. From the other side

of the desk, I leaned forward and tapped the wood surface with two fingers. "No one else has clearance to do shit like that." Except me, of course.

Pulling his hands together, he regrouped. I saw it happen. Like my father, he drew himself into a vid villain pose. "You do."

I raised my eyebrow. "You think I'd barge in here if I was behind it? Are you drunk, or high?"

"Vickie." He sighed with all the weight of the world on his shoulders. "Let's not play silly, childish games. I know you've been working on a BowerTech deal even though you said you're not. So you lied in an executive meeting."

"And what makes you so sure of that?"

"Malcolm told me to expect news on that front."

That didn't sound like Dad to me. He'd expect me to wait and tell him when he got back. "Did he?" I sat on the edge of the desk. Just two colleagues, chatting about the possibility of each other's traitorous behavior.

"He did. Thing is, I noticed you've set up a facility like you're expecting them."

Great. He'd poked around in my department. "And you're sure that's what it's for. Beyond a shadow of a doubt. Because there's no other possible explanation. And, of course, what my department does or doesn't do is completely your business."

"You're right. What you do with your department's budget is Malcolm's problem, not mine." He stood and buttoned his jacket. "We will, of course, have an executive team meeting this Friday, but I'm sure no one cares if you're squandering company resources."

He stepped around his desk. I hopped to my feet. This meeting had plowed off the rails and I needed to wrestle it into my control again.

"You made a deal with BowerTech," I said, choosing not to make it question.

Closing the distance between us, he smirked. "Who are you seeing?"

"None of your business."

He leaned in, forcing me against the desk. "Whoever they are, they aren't as good a match for you as I am."

"Not full of yourself or anything, though."

Grinning, he planted his hands on the desk, boxing me in. "Agree to marry me or I'll tell the directors you've embezzled millions through a subsidiary."

I blinked at him. Not only had I not done anything of the sort, I hadn't seen this coming. Mild panic pressed on me, brought on by the memory of his breath Saturday night. "What?"

"Big, bad Vickie." He pressed close and dropped his voice to a murmur. "The master of getting things done. Little does everyone realize she's lining her own pockets on the side while she works her mysterious magic. Oh, and by the way, she's been breaking the law left and right to do their dirty work. I'm sure the board will love that."

The fear from the other night raised my arms and shoved against him. "Yes, they love it when a man embarrasses himself by lying to them. It's endearing. Get off me."

He let go and stepped back with a grin. "It's not a lie if I can prove it."

I needed to leave the office as soon as possible and find a witness. Ross wouldn't do anything in front of Viola or Brad. "It's not proof if I can refute it." Flinging the door open burst a dam holding tension in my shoulders. Outside this office, I was safe.

Ross followed me out. He stuck his hands into his pants pockets and paced me as I nodded to Viola and hurried down the hall.

"Don't make the mistake of thinking I don't know what's going on. You and Malcolm have a lot of secrets. Be a shame if they popped out into the open."

"It would also be a shame if the Board decided to fire you. A crying shame."

He snorted. We reached Brad's workstation. I had no intention of entering my office with Ross harassing me this much.

"Who's this?" Ross said as I stopped to pretend I needed Brad for something.

"My new secretary, Brad. Brad, this is Mr. Lynch."

Brad smiled with innocence in need of crushing and offered Ross a hand to shake. "Nice to meet you, Mr. Lynch."

Ross ignored Brad's hand. Typical. "What happened to Marie?"

"She got a better offer," I said with a shrug.

Watching me through a calculating squint, Ross said, "Hasn't she been your secretary for over a decade?"

"The fuck do you care? My employees are my business." I jabbed a finger at him. "Just keep in mind that whatever you try with the board, I can counter it. Because my vote counts for more than yours, and it always will." The moment I said those words, I wanted to take them back. Ross couldn't get a majority stake in the company, but he could prevent me from doing so. He could also convince Dad I needed to step aside for a wide variety of reasons Dad might agree with.

Ross rolled his eyes and stalked away. I messaged Marie.

[VictoriaGodhand: I want to own 51% of our stock by the end of the week. Sooner is better.]

[MarieSclavo: That's really Brad's job now. I'll help him take care of it for you. But you need to start messaging him with this sort of thing.]

[VictoriaGodhand: Thank you.]

# CHAPTER 11

"Senator Gates scheduled the confirmation vote for today," Marie said. "He was able to avoid hearings, and expects to have good news around three-fifteen." Today, for the first time in forever, she wore something other than a suit or lingerie. Her floral-print sundress left her shoulders bare and flattered her curves.

I sipped coffee, watching rain through the bedroom window with my arms around Marie. The Ross situation had consumed me for the past few hours. Between me and the company, I couldn't tell which he wanted more. Dealing with him took more effort and energy than I wanted to admit because I didn't understand his motivations. Greed or lust? It made a difference.

"Good."

"Would you like me to order a celebratory dinner?"

"I feel like I need to have a meeting with security right

away to let them know," I said. "But maybe it should wait for tomorrow."

"No, do that," Marie said. She leaned her head against my shoulder. "We'll have dinner after. I'll get pizza and cake."

I laughed. "If that's what you want."

"You're going to tell Brad to set up that meeting. I'll take care of the food."

"Because as of that vote, you're officially laid off. And then you get laid."

"And then I get knocked up." She kissed the tip of my nose. "When?"

"Whenever you want, but Dad has to be able to go to the ceremony."

"Next week." Marie slipped out of my arms and bustled into the bathroom as if she needed to apply makeup and put on her dress already.

[MarieSclavo: I'll make the appointment during lunch so we can all go eat afterward. You're going to wear something nice.]

[VictoriaGodhand: Yes, dear.]

[MarieSclavo: I like the way that looks. Say it again.]

[VictoriaGodhand: Yes, dear. Whatever you say.]

[MarieSclavo: Shivers. I'm getting shivers. Can you

take a long lunch and entertain me until the vote is announced?]

She already knew the answer, and she'd already put a smile on my face. I wanted to continue to indulge, but I'd spent long enough here.

[VictoriaGodhand: I need to do the working thing. Enjoy yourself. But not too much.]

The hours dragged by. Lunch became a bright spot when Brad and Marie conspired to plan the wedding and lunch for next week while I said nothing. They put their heads together and made things happen. I knew how to manage projects and people, but they knew how to make the details sit up and beg.

I left my office at ten after three with a smile to sit with our VP of Security and a handful of his top people. On the way, Marie messaged to inform me she'd received confirmation the vote had gone through. That let me walk into my meeting with a broad smile. With eight people I knew by name, most of whom I'd helped hire, I discussed the security ramifications of our new status. They'd been anticipating this for months, but still had questions.

As I shook hands with everyone at the end of the meeting, I messaged Brad.

[VictoriaGodhand: I'm done for today, so you can go.]

[BradKleve: Yay! Marie went to fetch your dinner from the delivery service. Have fun, and see you tomorrow.]

His delight made me snort. On my way to the elevator a few minutes later, I messaged Marie next.

[VictoriaGodhand: We're done here. I'll be up shortly. Already sent Brad home, so you don't have to.]

She didn't respond, but I hadn't asked a question. The doors opened. Viola wasn't at her station, but something else sat on her desk—takeout boxes. One seemed the right shape for a pizza, and the other could hold anything, but as I approached, I thought it smelled like cake. My gaze snapped to the office door.

I imagined Marie walking past. Ross noticed.

Ross had attacked me. Twice.

Marie hadn't answered my message.

Viola and Brad had already left.

I gripped the doorknob and tried it. Locked.

Panic surged in my gut and shot out to my fingers and toes in a wave of ice.

[VictoriaGodhand: Security override on Malcolm Godhand's office. Unlock door.]

[GodhandIIncSystem: Security override access denied.]

I blasted a message to all eight of the people I'd just left, demanding they open Dad's office door. While I waited forever, I jiggled the knob, thumped my shoulder into the door, and kept panicking. One of them messaged me, then the door swung open against my shoulder. I stumbled inside. My feet only kept me standing because I still held the doorknob.

Blood. Too much blood. Running water. Bare flesh. Torn clothes. Blood.

Someone lay across Dad's desk. She wore Marie's floral sundress. Dark, wet stains defiled the fabric, ruining its simplistic joy. Her leg dangled off the side, limp and still.

But it wasn't Marie. It couldn't be Marie. I didn't want to know. My feet shuffled across the office anyway.

"Poor thing," Ross said.

Startled, I jumped to the side and stared at him. Shirtless and with damp hair, he used a towel to dry his hands. He swaggered toward me.

"She struggled more than I expected."

My stomach churned.

"On the bright side, now there's nothing in the way

between you and me."

Many times in my life, I'd thought I felt rage. Those moments all paled compared to the seething, venomous hatred that flared in my heart. I had no words, only action.

I launched myself at him with a shriek. He reacted too slow. My fist connected with his jaw. I'd never punched anyone before. He spun and stumbled away from me.

My entire universe narrowed to the man who'd tried to rape me, pressure me, and undermine me, and now had murdered the most precious thing in the world to me.

Because she'd struggled more than he'd expected.

"Vickie, wait." He rubbed his face.

There would be no waiting. I raised my knee. He lurched aside. I hit his thigh. With this, he seemed to realize I wouldn't stop. Ross scrambled for the door. I dove to tackle him but missed. He ran to the elevator.

Beyond conscious thought, I scrabbled to my feet and chased after him. I hit the elevator doors as they closed and shoved my hand between them. Ross squeaked as the doors opened and I pounced on him. We rode the elevator in a flail of fists and feet.

The doors opened. Ross ran across the lobby. I chased him. My heels clacked.

"Miss Godhand?" Someone grabbed my shoulders.

I didn't see who had dared to interfere. Wriggling free, I grabbed his gun and pointed it at Ross. The crack of its report echoed. I flinched. Someone screamed. The glass wall behind him shattered, though it stayed in its frame.

I fired again. Ross's body twisted and he doubled over, but didn't fall. Why the fuck didn't this asshole fall? Stalking toward him, I fired again, hitting another glass wall. Ross raised his head and stared at me, eyes wide and skin pale. Blood stained his hand where he gripped his shoulder.

People shouted and screamed. He scrambled to flee. No way would this pile of shit escape. I ran and plowed into him. We crashed through an already shattered wall of glass. Shards of glass rained as we landed on plascrete. He grunted as he hit. I fell on top of him.

While he gathered his wits, I sat up and pressed the barrel of my gun to his head. Though I wanted to splatter his brains across the sidewalk for everyone to see, I also wanted him to suffer. I wanted to see him quiver with fear. He deserved a slow, horrible, painful death.

"Drop the gun!"

I looked up to see a gun barrel pointed at me. The sight made no sense.

"Miss Godhand," someone said. "Please put my gun down."

Twisting, I saw Dave, the security guard. He held his hands up, surrendering to me. Behind him, other guards watched, their faces stunned, shocked, or confused.

Ross gasped for breath. "You fucking bitch," he wheezed.

"Sir, please remain quiet." The man holding the gun on me wore a uniform. A cop pointed a gun at me.

"You have no authority here," I said, though my voice sounded empty. "We have extraterritoriality as of an hour ago."

"Ma'am, you're on a public sidewalk. Put down the gun and move away from that man."

"He killed Marie." My voice seemed small and faint as I started to grasp the situation. "He slit her throat. In my dad's office."

"Miss Godhand," Dave said again. "Please put down the gun. You don't want to murder Mr. Lynch on the sidewalk. I promise."

For a moment, I considered turning the gun on myself. But then Ross would live. He'd get everything he wanted. No matter what, I got nothing. If I lived, though, I could still make him pay.

I let Dave take his gun. The cop arrested me. Our security guards ignored Ross, lying on the sidewalk and bleeding from a gunshot wound in his shoulder. Instead, they watched the cop cuff me. Dave handed the gun to the cop and told him to take good care of me.

Pain flooded me. I collapsed into tears.

# CHAPTER 12

My Dad never showed up, but he sent lawyers. Later, I learned he'd been unable to catch a shuttle back to Earth before his scheduled departure. When he did return, he met with Ross on Monday morning, a few hours before my arraignment, then he disappeared on the way to the courthouse.

I didn't know how Ross managed to remove him without a trace, but I had suspicions. Without Dad there, I plead guilty on the advice of my lawyers. They had video of me sitting on Ross with a gun pressed to his temple. Though the shooting had taken place on private property outside police jurisdiction, they still charged me with attempted murder. All Marie's messages had become admissible with her death, and they had several of me saying I wanted to kill Ross.

My guilty plea meant only ten years in Auburn Detention Facility. I could reduce it with good behavior. In ten years, Ross could cause a lot of damage to and with the company. At least I still owned it. With my Dad's third of the stock as part of my inheritance, I owned seventy-five percent of the company.

Grief overwhelmed me for weeks. I didn't care about anything. ADF happened. Every moment of every day, I wished I'd shot Ross again instead of handing over the gun. At least then, Marie would've been avenged and Dad wouldn't have disappeared. After a few days, I settled into the routine. Nothing mattered anymore, except avoiding punishments and earning brownie points to get out sooner. The sooner I got out, the sooner I could have Ross killed by a professional who wouldn't miss with the first shot.

Because I had no contact with the outside world unless they came to visit in person.

"I'm so sorry about Marie and your dad." Brad sat across a table from me in a bare, stark room intended for lawyer visits. By law, no one could monitor or record the audio, but prison staff could record video the entire time. Compared to the conjugal visit rooms, where they could listen but not watch, I preferred this. He'd gained access to it by getting my lawyer to sign off on him as an assistant, at my request.

I didn't want to talk about either. If I didn't talk about it, I could avoid feeling anything. "Thanks."

"Ross demoted me to the secretarial pool. Jay said to expect that, so all your files were already wiped when he did it, with backups stashed in my apartment. At Ross's request, the Board of Directors has decided it's in the company's best interest to ignore the inconvenient fact that you own the company while you're in jail. They're going to ask you to consider doing a handoff of your stock."

"Great." If I agreed, I'd give up my voting power on the board. If I didn't agree, I had a feeling they'd try increasingly dickish options to push me out. My dad had built that company. It had our name.

"But the most important reason why I came is that Jay wants to talk to you. He said to tell you, and I quote, 'fuck the risk.' In my palm, I have a state-of-the-art, solar-powered jammer that will let you punch through the blocks here and message whoever you want without being monitored. That's all it does. The device doesn't have a battery, and it only works in direct sunlight, so outside on a sunny day. Best I could do. Anything bigger and the bribe to get it through security here would be outrageous."

"Pass it when we shake hands." Marie would've done

the same thing, though she would've managed it sooner.

"Yes. I just wanted to tell you first. Are you being treated...decently?"

"More or less." I closed my eyes and rubbed my temples. Trading sex for favors had come easily, of course. The normality of it had kept me on an even keel. "Thank you, Brad. You barely know me, but you're doing good work. I appreciate that."

"I really liked Marie. She would've wanted this. And Ross is an asshole who doesn't deserve what he's managed to get. Besides, your bank account has more than enough to keep me living well for a long damned time, and I'm pretty sure you're smart enough to find a way to keep me busy as your personal assistant for even longer than that."

I wished Brad had been able to keep his innocence. At least I knew I had his loyalty. "She liked you too." Still shying away from thoughts of her and my dad, I stood. "Keep your eyes and ears open."

"I will. Good luck in here. Message me anytime you need something."

We shook hands. He passed me the device, and I stuck my hands in my pockets. The guard outside opened the door and I watched my only connection to the outside world leave.

# CHAPTER 13

The sun beat down as I clipped the tiny solar-powered jammer to my ear. Sweat soaked the rough orange fabric of my jumpsuit. Dust from the exercise yard coated my throat. Everyone left me alone, a status I'd worked hard to achieve and appreciated. Even three months after her death, the image of Marie covered in blood lingered in my mind, impossible to banish.

[VictoriaGodhandSystem: WAINet connection established. Unable to sync at this time. Connection abnormality detected. Messages may not be transmitted as intended.]

I sighed and hoped Brad had given me the right thing. My first message went to Jay, because I had no one else anymore.

[VictoriaGodhand: Yep, fuck the risk.]

[JaySmith: Why the fuck didn't you come to me?]

I sighed and wished for the thousandth time that I'd done so many things differently.

[VictoriaGodhand: It happened too fast. I didn't think.]

[JaySmith: I can't get you out of jail right now. I don't have the crew for that. Maybe while you were in holding, but Brad wouldn't authorize payment until he heard from you, and my people wouldn't do it for less than half upfront. Now you're in ADF, and that's next level shit. It's gonna have to wait until I can get some specialized help and a fucking plan.]

For some reason, I'd expected him to be capable of miracles. His shortcomings made this wretched place feel more like a prison than it had two minutes ago.

[VictoriaGodhand: I understand.]

[JaySmith: Ross is a piece of work.]

[VictoriaGodhand: That's one way to put it.]

[JaySmith: You know what would be easier than breaking you out of jail? Killing Ross. Like, a lot easier. I have a few people who've worked for you before lined up and ready to take that mission. All I need is your approval and a deposit.]

He sent me the price, which seemed low. Without

hesitation, I messaged Brad to approve the transfer with instructions on how to handle the mission from his end.

[VictoriaGodhand: Fucking do it. Make sure he suffers. I want him helpless and begging before he dies. Put him through hell.]

[JaySmith: Yes ma'am. I'll get you the video the next time you connect.]

That night, for the first time in a long while, I slept well.

# Other Books by the Author

**Darkside Seattle**
gritty cyberpunk
*Street Doc*
*Fixer*
*Mechanic* (coming in late 2017)

**Maze Beset trilogy**
superheroes in denim
*Dragons In Pieces*
*Dragons In Chains*
*Dragons In Flight*

**Spirit Knights series**
young adult urban fantasy
*Girls Can't Be Knights*
*Backyard Dragons*
*Ethereal Entanglements*
*Ghost is the New Normal*

**Tales of Ilauris**
sword & sorcery fantasy
*Damsel In Distress*
*Shadow & Spice*
*Al-Kabar*

## The Greatest Sin series
epic snark fantasy
co-authored with Erik Kort
*The Fallen*
*Harbinger*
*Moon Shades*
*Illusive Echoes*
*A Curse of Memories*

## Non-fiction
co-authored with Jeffrey Cook
*Working the Table: An Indie Author's Guide to Conventions*

## Anthologies
*Into the Woods: a fantasy anthology*
*Merely This and Nothing More: Poe Goes Punk*
*Unnatural Dragons: a science fiction anthology*
*Missing Pieces VII*
*Artifact*
*What We've Unlearned: English Class Goes Punk*
*Bridges* (Editor)

# About the Author

L.E. French is the cyberpunk pseudonym of Lee French, a fantasy and superhero author. She lives in Olympia, WA with two kids, two bicycles, and too much stuff. An avid gamer, compulsive writer, and casual cyclist, she can often be found on myth-weavers.com, sitting in her BeanBag of Inspiration +4, or riding her bike around the city.

She is an active member of SFWA, the Science Fiction and Fantasy Writers of America (www.sfwa.org) and NIWA, the Northwest Independent Writers Association, as well as serving the Olympia NaNoWriMo region as a Municipal Liason.

Made in the USA
Columbia, SC
10 February 2018